Big Red and the Little Bitty Wolf

A Story About Bullying

by Jeanie Franz Ransom • illustrated by Jennifer Zivoin

Magination Press • Washington, DC • American Psychological Association

To my wise friend, Mr. Know-it-Owl—*JFR*

To Olivia and Elyse, for all the big and little bitty smiles that brighten every day—*JZ*

Published by
MAGINATION PRESS®
An Educational Publishing Foundation Book
American Psychological Association
750 First Street NE
Washington, DC 20002

Magination Press is a registered trademark of the American Psychological Association.

For more information about our books, including a complete catalog, please write to us, call 1-800-374-2721, or visit our website at www.apa.org/pubs/magination.

Book design by Gwen Grafft
Printed by Lake Book Manufacturing, Inc., Melrose Park, IL

Names: Ransom, Jeanie Franz, 1957– author. | Zivoin, Jennifer, illustrator.
Title: Big Red and the Little Bitty Wolf : a story about bullying /
by Jeanie Franz Ransom ; illustrated by Jennifer Zivoin.
Description: Washington, DC : Magination Press, 2016. |
  Summary: Big Red Riding Hood has been bullying Little Bitty Wolf
  since she moved into the neighborhood and his parents' advice does
  not help, but their school counselor, Mr. Know-It-Owl, makes a
  comment that just might set things right.
Identifiers: LCCN 2015016046 | ISBN 9781433820489 (hardcover) |
  ISBN 143382048X (hardcover)
Subjects: | CYAC: Bullying—Fiction. | Wolves—Fiction. |
  Characters in Literature—Fiction.
Classification: LCC PZ7.R1744 Big 2016 |
  DDC [E]—dc23 LC record available at http://lccn.loc.gov/2015016046

Manufactured in the
United States of America
First printing October 2015
10 9 8 7 6 5 4 3 2 1

There was only one path that led from where Little Bitty Wolf
lived to where he went to school at Pine Cone Elementary.
And that was a problem.

Over the summer, Big Red Riding Hood had moved in with her
grandmother. Big Red wasn't just big. She was mean. And now
she took the same path through the woods to get to school.

Before Big Red moved in, Little Bitty
loved to go to school. He loved the soft
pad-pad-pad sound his paws made on the
path. He loved the feel of the wind tickling
his whiskers as it rustled the leaves.

And he really, really loved his yellow
lunch basket, always packed
with his favorite foods.

Big Red loved nothing more than teasing, taunting, and terrorizing Little Bitty.

Sometimes she jumped out from behind a tree.

Sometimes she stuck out her big foot and tripped him.

Sometimes Big Red snuck up behind Little Bitty and pulled his tail.

Little Bitty tried not to whine.

He tried not to whimper.

He tried not to talk to Big Red at all.

Nothing seemed to help.
Little Bitty asked his parents what to do.

"Just tell her to stop," Mom told him.
"Tell her you don't like it when she teases you."

"Stop it!" Little Bitty said when
Big Red kept throwing
acorns at him. "I don't like that!"
Big Red laughed.

"But I do," Big Red said.
And she picked up a big acorn
and hit him in the nose.

"Puff yourself up so you'll look bigger," Dad told him.

So the next time Big Red pulled his tail, Little Bitty puffed himself up as big as he could.

But Big Red just laughed.
"I'm not scared of a
little bitty wolf," she smirked.

Little Bitty didn't know what to do. And then one morning,
a shadow fell across the path. Little Bitty looked up. It was Big Red.

"Where do you think you're going?" Big Red asked.

Little Bitty tried to run by Big Red, but she blocked his way.
"Not so fast."

Big Red grabbed the basket right out of his paws and skipped away.
"A-tisket, a-tasket, I've got a brand new basket."

Little Bitty was so sad. What would he eat for lunch?
What would his parents say when he didn't
bring his basket home? Would they make him
take his food in a brown-bark bag?

When Little Bitty Wolf got to school, his teacher,
Ms. Doe, asked what was wrong. Little Bitty
didn't want to tell her. Big Red was looking right at him.

Ms. Doe sent him to talk to the school counselor, Mr. Know-It-Owl.
Little Bitty Wolf told him about Big Red.

"It sounds like quite a problem," Mr. Know-It-Owl said.
"What have you tried to fix it?"

"I asked Big Red to stop bothering me, just like my mom said,"
Little Bitty told the counselor. "And I puffed myself up
to look bigger, just like my dad told me," said Little Bitty.
"But Big Red just laughed at me. And now she has my lunch basket
and I don't know what to do!" He wiped his eyes with his tail.

"Seems to me you need to do something Big Red doesn't expect you to do," Mr. Know-It-Owl said. "Like this!" Mr. Know-It-Owl's head spun all the way around.

Little Bitty smiled.

"My, what a nice smile you have," Mr. Know-It-Owl told him. "I never noticed before. You should smile more often."

Little Bitty decided he would do just that.

On the way home from school, when Big Red jumped out from behind a tree, Little Bitty didn't whimper. He didn't whine. He just smiled.

"Are you smiling at me?" Big Red asked. "What's going on?"

Little Bitty just kept smiling. He was so nervous, it was all he could do to keep his paws planted in one place.

"What's so funny?" Big Red asked, taking a step back.
"Stop looking at me like that! What are you going to do, bite me?"
Little Bitty Wolf laughed. What a silly thing to say.
Biting was for babies!

"You can have your dumb old basket back," Big Red said.
"I didn't want it anyway!" She tossed the basket on the ground.

Little Bitty smiled even bigger. Mr. Know-It-Owl
was right. Doing something Big Red didn't
expect had worked. Maybe he'd never smiled at
her before. He had a feeling Big Red didn't get many
smiles. He'd make sure she got plenty now.

Little Bitty trotted off toward
home with his ears up and
his tail high, feeling a little bit
bigger and a whole lot better.

Note to Parents and Caregivers
by Elizabeth McCallum, PhD

In recent years, the media, educators, and researchers have paid increased attention to the epidemic of childhood bullying in an effort to reduce and prevent bullying behaviors. Bullying is defined as a type of aggressive behavior involving an imbalance of power between perpetrator and victim that occurs repeatedly with the intention to cause harm. Bullying can take several forms, including physical, verbal, and social harassment. Bullying is associated with a variety of long-term negative outcomes for both victims and perpetrators, including depression, anxiety, academic failure, criminal activity, and even suicide.

While a national conversation about the dangers of bullying has begun and many schools have adopted curricula aimed specifically at bullying prevention, many students continue to struggle with bullying in schools. In fact, recent statistics report that as many as one in four school-aged children has been the victim of bullying.

HOW THIS BOOK CAN HELP

Big Red and the Little Bitty Wolf provides an interesting twist on the classic story Little Red Riding Hood in which the tables are turned and Little Bitty Wolf comes up against Big Red on his way to school each day.

Reading this book with your child can be a way to spark a more in-depth discussion about the widespread issue of childhood bullying and the feelings associated with it. By discussing both Little Bitty Wolf and Big Red's thoughts and feelings about being the victim or perpetrator of bullying, children may be more likely to engage in conversation about their own feelings about this issue.

HOW TO HELP YOUR CHILD

If you are a parent concerned about bullying, it is important to understand common signs indicating that a child is involved in bullying as well as actions that can be taken to improve the situation. Bullying can have long-lasting negative effects on victims, perpetrators, and bystanders.

Taking a stand against bullying involves being committed to providing a safe environment characterized by respect for the dignity of all human beings. The following sections offer warning signs for parents to look out for, as well as actions that can be taken if you believe your child is involved in bullying.

If Your Child Is the Victim of Bullying

Often, victims of bullying feel shame and embarrassment and do not report the bullying to parents or authorities. Therefore, the first step in helping a child who is the victim of bullying is to know the warning signs associated with bullying. Common warning signs that a child is being bullied include:

- Lost, missing, or damaged clothing or other belongings upon returning home from school
- Unexplained cuts, scrapes, or bruises
- Changes in sleeping habits or appetite
- Anxiety over going to school or other organized activities
- Loss of interest in previously preferred activities
- Moodiness, frequent crying, or other signs of depression
- Complaints of headaches, stomachaches, or other physical problems that cannot be otherwise explained
- Loss of interest in school
- Sudden decrease in academic performance

If you believe your child is the victim of bullying, the following are steps you can take to help your child and stop the bullying:

- Talk to your child's teacher or principal about what is going on and work closely with the school to help solve the problem.
- Encourage your child to talk about his or her bullying experiences. Empathize with your child and let him or her know that the bullying is wrong and it is not your child's fault.
- Teach your child nonviolent ways of dealing with the bullying, like walking away or playing with friends. Encourage your child to interact with friendly peers in school or help your child make friends somewhere outside of school.
- Teach your child strategies to ensure his or her safety, particularly informing an adult of instances of bullying.

- Don't encourage your child to retaliate. This could lead to him or her getting hurt or an increase in the frequency and intensity of the bullying.
- Encourage your child to get involved in interests and hobbies outside of school. This will help your child develop resilience and social skills that may be used in instances of bullying.
- Ensure that your child's home environment is safe and loving. All children need warmth and stability at home, but this is particularly important for children enduring harassment and the associated fears and anxiety at school.

If Your Child Is the Perpetrator of Bullying

Parents should also know the warning signs of a child who may be a perpetrator of bullying. These include:

- Difficulty controlling anger
- Rough or aggressive behavior during play
- Friendship with peers who are bullies
- Low tolerance for frustration
- Intimidating smaller or younger children
- Opposition toward adults
- Getting into trouble at school

If you believe your child may be the perpetrator of bullying, the following are steps you can take to help your child:

- Be absolutely clear that bullying is a serious issue and that it will not be tolerated.
- Set house rules for appropriate behavior and hold your child accountable for following these rules. Additionally, specify what the consequences of bullying will be and enforce them. Reward your child for resolving conflicts in a nonviolent way.
- Monitor your child's behaviors closely and be aware of who his or her friends are. Know how and where they spend their time.
- Encourage your child to become involved in a preferred activity or hobby. This will help build self-esteem and encourage positive social skills learned and practiced through the activity.
- Work closely with your child's school to ensure that your child

receives a consistent message that bullying is not acceptable and will lead to negative consequences.

If Your Child Witnesses Bullying

Bullying bystanders are people who observe or hear about the act of bullying without being the perpetrator or the victim. Recent research has focused on the role bystanders can play in improving the situation. The "helpful bystander" is an individual who supports the victim by standing up to the bullying or reporting the bullying to an adult.

The following are steps you can take to help your child be a "helpful bystander":

- Encourage your child to feel empathy for the victim. You can do this by helping your child imagine how the bullied child might feel about being bullied and about bystanders not offering assistance.
- Model respect and kindness at home. If your child sees you acting respectfully toward others, he or she will be likely to follow suit.
- Set high standards and expectations for your child's behavior and praise him or her for positive actions, particularly those that demonstrate support and empathy for others.
- Communicate to your child that without an audience of bystanders, bullying is less likely to occur.
- Encourage your child to be helpful by stepping in and supporting the victim or notifying an adult about what's going on.

Whether your child is a victim, perpetrator, or bystander of bullying, if your child seems to be experiencing particular emotional distress, it may be helpful to seek consultation from your child's school mental health counselor, or a licensed psychologist or psychotherapist.

Elizabeth McCallum, PhD, is an associate professor in the school psychology program at Duquesne University, as well as a Pennsylvania certified school psychologist. She is the author of many scholarly journal articles and book chapters on topics including academic and behavioral interventions for children and adolescents.

ABOUT THE AUTHOR

Jeanie Franz Ransom is a licensed professional counselor whose books include *Don't Squeal Unless It's a Big Deal, I Don't Want to Talk About It,* and *What Really Happened to Humpty?* She's also worked as an elementary school counselor, where she was never without her popular puppet, Mr. Know-It-Owl. Jeanie and her husband are parents to three grown boys and two dogs, and divide their time between St. Louis, MO, and Northport, MI.

ABOUT THE ILLUSTRATOR

Jennifer Zivoin has always loved art and storytelling, so becoming an illustrator was a natural career path. She has been trained in media ranging from figure drawing to virtual reality, and earned her bachelor of arts degree with highest distinction from the honors division of Indiana University. During her professional career, Jennifer worked as a graphic designer and then as a creative director before finding her artistic niche illustrating children's books. In addition to artwork, she enjoys reading, cooking, and ballroom dancing. Jennifer lives in Indiana with her family.

ABOUT MAGINATION PRESS

Magination Press is an imprint of the American Psychological Association, the largest scientific and professional organization representing psychologists in the United States and the largest association of psychologists worldwide.